I belong to
THE BEST BOOK CLUB EVER™
This is my book.

My name is

..............................................................

Will you please read it to me?

# Seven in One Blow

A Random House PICTUREBACK®

Freire Wright & Michael Foreman's

# Seven in One Blow

RANDOM HOUSE 🏠 NEW YORK

Copyright © 1978 by Michael Foreman and Freire Wright. All rights reserved under International and Pan-American Copyright Conventions. Published in the United States by Random House, Inc., New York, and simultaneously in Canada by Random House of Canada Limited, Toronto. Library of Congress Catalog Card Number: 77-92379. ISBN: 0-394-83804-1 (B.C.); 0-394-83805-X (trade). Manufactured in the United States of America. CDEFGHIJ 1234567890

One day a little tailor sat busily sewing in his shop. While he was sewing, a swarm of flies landed on the bread and jam he had set aside for lunch. "Shoo! Shoo!" said the tailor angrily.

But the flies just buzzed louder as they ate the sweet jam.

"Take that!" the little tailor cried, and he swatted at the flies with a piece of cloth.

To his surprise, seven flies fell down dead. "Well," he said, quite pleased with himself. "I've killed seven in one blow!"

The little tailor was so proud of his feat that he made
a belt that said SEVEN IN ONE BLOW. Then he went
out into the world to seek his fortune.

He put on his belt, closed his shop, and bought a piece
of cheese to put in his pocket for supper.

When he reached the edge of town, the tailor heard a chirping sound. On the ground was a little bird, which he put into his pocket.

"A bird will be good company for me on my journey," he said as he strode merrily down the road.

Soon the tailor met a giant. "Good day," said the tailor cheerfully.

"Be off with you," the giant roared, "or I won't let you leave in one piece!"

"I see you don't know who I am," said the tailor. And he stepped back so the giant could read the words on his belt.

The giant thought the tailor had killed seven men. *"Seven in one blow!"* he cried, feeling sorry he had been so rude.

"Let's see just how strong you are,"
said the giant. He picked up a stone
and squeezed it so hard that a drop of water
came from it. "Try that!" he exclaimed.

The tailor thought quickly. Pretending
to pick up a stone, he brought out his piece
of cheese instead and squeezed it until the whey
ran out. "That was easy enough," he said.

"Hm-m," said the puzzled giant. "Try this, then." He picked up another stone and threw it so far that it almost disappeared from sight.

"That's simple," said the tailor. Quickly he took the little bird from his pocket. Before the giant could see what it was, he threw the bird into the air. Off it flew, right out of sight.

"Here's something I'm sure you can't do," said the giant.
"Help me carry this fallen tree back to my castle."
"No trouble at all," said the little tailor.

With a grunt the giant lifted the tree trunk and trudged off.
While the giant huffed and puffed under the heavy load, the clever
tailor sat in the branches as comfortable as he could be.

Soon the giant had to sit down and rest. The little tailor hopped out of the branches and pretended he had been helping. "Tired out from such easy work?" he asked.

The giant tried to hide his anger. "Though you are small, you do seem strong," he said slyly. "Come home with me and meet my brothers."

So the little tailor went off to meet the giant's six brothers.

The giants all laughed loudly when the tailor told them how he had beaten their brother. And after giving him an enormous supper, they showed him to his room. But the bed was much too big for the little tailor. So he curled up to sleep on the rug.

Late that night, two of the giants crept up to the tailor's room.

They pounded his bed with huge clubs.
"That is the end of the little scalawag!"
they said.

The loud pounding woke the tailor. He crept out of his room and overheard the two giants boasting that they had killed him in his bed.

After the giants were asleep again, the tailor sneaked along the wall and dropped an apple on one giant's head.

"Why did you hit me?" the giant shouted. And he gave the closest brother a hard poke.

The tailor dropped another apple. It hit a third giant, who immediately struck a fourth brother on the nose.

Before long a brawl had begun. Safely perched on top of the wall, the tailor watched the giants fight.

They kept at it until they had knocked each other out.
The little tailor tied them all up, then set out once
more in search of his fortune.

By morning the tailor arrived at a city, where the people were rushing around in a frenzy. Soldiers were everywhere.

"What is all the commotion about?" asked the little tailor.

"Giants!" replied a soldier. "They are robbing travelers, destroying our homes, and eating up all our cattle! Those giants have caused so much trouble that the king has promised his daughter's hand in marriage to anyone who can get rid of them."

"Well, you needn't worry about giants any more," said the little tailor, "for I've just finished off a whole castleful of them."

The soldiers could scarcely believe the little tailor's story. But they finally took him to see the king.

"You?" scoffed the king. "How could a little fellow like you beat the giants? My bravest soldiers have failed to do so."

As for the princess, she liked the little tailor so much she was ready to believe anything.

"Come with me and you can see for yourself, Your Majesty," said the tailor. And he led the king, the soldiers, and the townspeople to the giants' castle.

When the king saw the great pile of giants, bound hand and foot, he exclaimed, "Why, this looks like the work of a hundred men!"

The giants were banished from the land...

...and the little tailor warned them never to return—or next time he would thrash them even more soundly.

So the little tailor and the princess were married
that very day. All the townspeople rejoiced and
called out, "Hurrah for the brave little tailor!"

The little tailor lived on in the castle, and he had much good fortune.

And just to remind himself of how it had all come about, the tailor always wore the belt that said SEVEN IN ONE BLOW.

Thank you.